Jerome Camps Out

Written and Illustrated by

EILEEN CHRISTELOW

Clarion Books/New York

FOR JENNY WHITE,
GOOD FRIEND
AND NEIGHBOR!

Clarion Books • a Houghton Mifflin Company imprint • 215 Park Avenue South, New York, NY 10003 •
Copyright © 1998 by Eileen Christelow • Illustrations executed in pen, ink, and watercolors. • Text is
14-point Daily News. • All rights reserved. • For information about permission to reproduce selections from
this book, write to Permissions, Houghton Mifflin Company, 215 Park Avenue South, New York, NY 10003.
• Printed in the USA • **Library of Congress Cataloging-in-Publication Data** • Christelow, Eileen. • Jerome
camps out / by Eileen Christelow • p.   cm. • Summary: Jerome the alligator is looking forward to the
Swamp School camping trip, until he and his friend learn that Buster, the class bully, will be there, too. •
ISBN: 0-395-75831-9 PA ISBN: 0-618-19467-3 • [1. Alligators—Fiction. 2. Bullies—Fiction. 3. Camps—
Fiction.] I. Title. • PZ7.C4523Jd 1998 • [E]—dc21 97-24024 • CIP AC • WOZ 10 9 8 7 6 5 4 3

Jerome was almost packed for the Swamp School camping trip. His friend P.J. was waiting for him.

"This is going to be the best-ever weekend!" said Jerome. "Swimming, fishing, hiking . . ."

"It might be the worst-ever weekend," said P.J. "Don't forget, we have to share a tent with Buster Wormley. He put ants in my lunch box four times last week."

"If Buster tries anything funny, just ignore him," said Jerome.

Jerome and P.J. walked over to Swamp School to meet the bus to the campsite.

"If we stick together, Buster won't bother us," said Jerome. "So why worry?"

"I'm worried," said P.J.

When they got to school, Buster was already there.
"Quick!" whispered P.J. "Head for the bus before he sees us!"

But they were too late.

"Nice hat!" said Buster.

"Give it back!" shouted Jerome.

"Try to make me," said Buster, "and I'll turn you into lime jelly!"

On the bus, their friend Gloria whispered, "Why don't you slug Buster and take back your hat!"

"I'm not that crazy. It's only a stupid hat," said Jerome.

When the bus parked at the campsite, everyone headed for the river.

Jerome and P.J. tried to steer clear of Buster.

But it wasn't easy.

It took imagination to avoid Buster.

"If you think you have problems now," said Gloria, "wait until tonight. It will be just the two of you and Buster in one little tent. You won't be able to hide then."

"Maybe we could sleep in a different tent," said Jerome. "The teachers would never notice."

But that night, Miss Gator noticed. "You boys must be lost," she said. "Aren't you supposed to be with Buster?"

"We're doomed," sighed P.J. as they carried their packs to their tent.

"Don't worry!" said Jerome. "Buster is probably asleep by now."

"I'm worried," said P.J.

Buster was not asleep. "You twerps can squeeze into that corner," he said. "But don't step on my snakes."

"Snakes?" yelled P.J. "I'm getting out of here!"

"Wait for me!" said Jerome.

Jerome and P.J. set up their sleeping bags behind a bush and put on their pajamas. "I'll bet they were rubber snakes," said Jerome.

"Who cares?" said P.J. "I'm not taking any chances."

"Well, don't worry. Buster won't bother us out here," said Jerome.

"I'm worried," said P.J.

When Jerome and P.J. woke up the next morning, their clothes and backpacks were gone. They couldn't find them anywhere.

"I knew we should worry," said P.J.

"You boys ought to keep better track of your things," said Miss Gator. "Now you'll have to go hiking in your pajamas."

"You guys look really cute," sneered Buster as they started out on the hike.

"I'd flatten Buster," whispered Gloria.

"I'd rather get home alive," said Jerome.

"Sh-h-h!" said Miss Gator. She was peering through her binoculars. "Look! Up in that tree! Is that a bird . . . with blue stripes?"

Everyone looked.

"That's my shirt!" gasped Jerome.

"There's my pants!" groaned P.J.

"Now, just how did your clothes get up there?" asked Miss Gator.

"Maybe a big bird put them there," suggested Buster.

Jerome and P.J. had to rescue their clothes while everyone else went on the hike.

"We should buy Buster a one-way ticket to the moon," grumbled P.J.

"I have a better plan," said Jerome.

Jerome and P.J. had to work quickly before everyone came back from the hike.

"All we need is some monster footprints coming out of the lake," said Jerome.

"I hope this works," said P.J.

"It will," said Jerome. "Especially if Gloria helps."

That evening, they let Gloria in on the plan.

"You can count on me," said Gloria. "My monster imitation terrifies everyone. Just give me a few minutes to run into the woods."

"Hurry!" whispered P.J. "Here comes Buster!"

Gloria ran off as Buster came down the path.

"What are you twerps doing?" asked Buster.

"Look at these huge footprints," said Jerome. "They might be from that Deep Lake monster!"

"Oh sure," said Buster. "What Deep Lake monster?"

"It has huge teeth and glowing eyes and it screams and shrieks!" said P.J. "I sure don't want to meet up with it!"

"It wouldn't bother me," said Buster.

Just then they heard sticks snapping and leaves crunching and a loud shriek from the woods.

"What's that?" gasped Buster.

"Head for the tent!" whispered Jerome.

They all ran. Buster got to the tent first.

Buster huddled under his sleeping bag. Heavy footsteps shuffled toward them.

"Sh-h-h! Don't move!" whispered Jerome. "It's coming this way!"

A large shadow hovered over the tent.

"Help!" squealed Buster.

"Shhh!" hissed P.J.

A short time later, the footsteps moved away toward the woods.

"That was close," said Jerome.

"Is it gone?" whispered Buster.
Jerome and P.J. peeked out of the tent.
"It's gone," said Jerome.
"So you'll be okay here alone," said P.J.
"ALONE?" gasped Buster.

"You don't need us," said Jerome.

"I might," said Buster.

"Your snakes will protect you," said P.J.

"That was a joke!" said Buster. "They aren't real!"

"That's too bad," said Jerome. "We're still leaving."

"If you stay, I'll give back your hat!" said Buster. "I'll do anything!"

"Maybe we should stay," said P.J.

"This is more like it," said Jerome as he settled into his sleeping bag. "Tonight we should get some sleep."

"How can you sleep?" said Buster. "Suppose that thing comes back?"

"I'm not worried," said P.J. as he closed his eyes.

The next morning, the Swamp School kids headed home on the bus.

"I'm never going back there!" said Buster. "That monster kept me up all night!" Then he fell fast asleep.

"What monster?" whispered Gloria. "I couldn't help out last night."

"But you did," said Jerome. "Didn't you?"

"No!" said Gloria. "Miss Gator caught me sneaking into the woods."

"Then what was that noise we heard? And what was walking around our tent?" gasped P.J.

"I don't even want to think about it!" said Jerome.